ROUND IS A PANCAKE

by Joan Sullivan Baranski

illustrated by Yu-Mei Han

DUTTON CHILDREN'S BOOKS
NEW YORK

Round is a pancake,

round is a plum.

Round is a doughnut

and the top of a drum.

ringing out loud.

Round are the cartwheels

they spin through the crowd.

Round is
a lollipop,

round is
a ring.

Round is a button

and the crown of a king.

Round is a birds' nest,

round is a wheel.

Round is a daisy

and a fisherman's reel.

Round is a coin,

round is a cake.

Round is a cherry

and the cookies we bake.

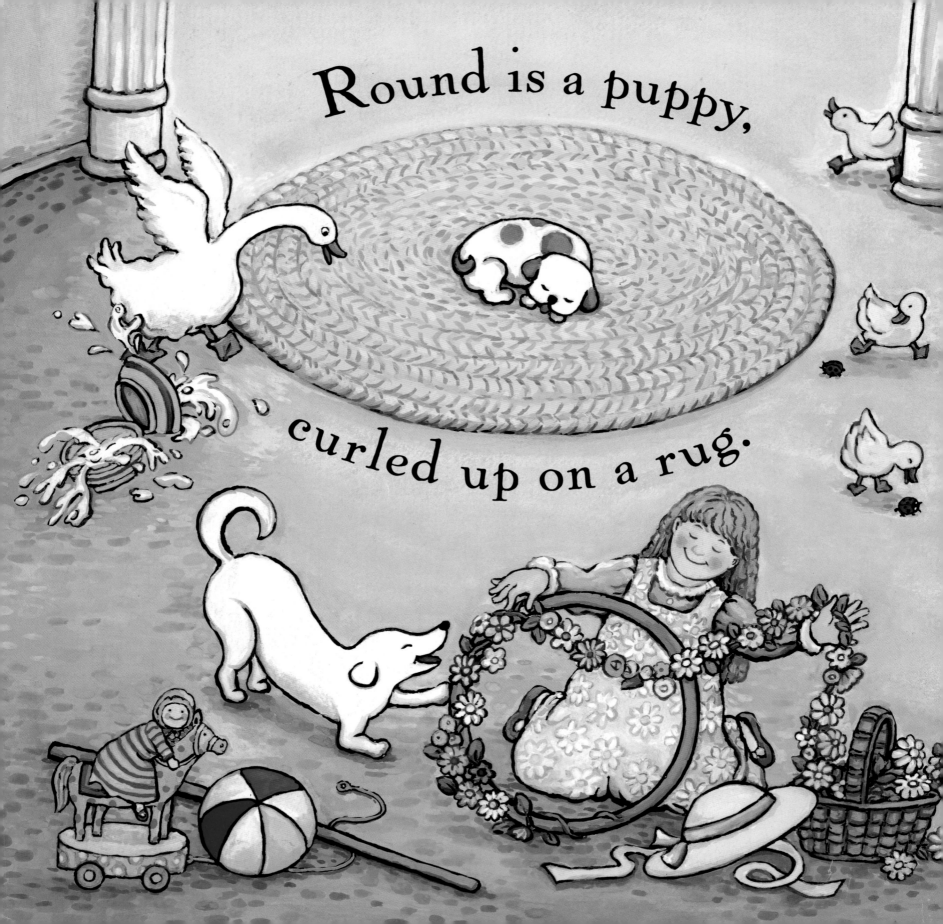

Round is a puppy, curled up on a rug.

Round are the spots

on a wee ladybug.

Look all around you:

on the ground,

In the air.

To the memory of my dear father—Shih-Chi Han
Y. M. H.

CIP Data is available.

Published in the United States by Dutton Children's Books,

a division of Penguin Putnam Books for Young Readers

345 Hudson Street, New York, New York 10014

www.penguinputnam.com

Designed by Alan Carr

ISBN 0-525-46173-6

Printed in Hong Kong · First Edition

1 3 5 7 9 10 8 6 4 2